Also by Rachael Reed

Codefendant

Codefendant

Once a Cheater

Once a Cheater

Passport Bro

What Happens in Prison

Preference

Sprinkle Sprinkle

Championship Bad

Street Exodus

Street Exodus

Street Royalty

Pawns of Power

SIS

Cartel Bloodline

Get Money Girls

Skip the Games

Til Death Do Us Part

Backpage Hustle

Skip The Games

Rachael Reed
©2024

Skip The Games

By Rachael Reed

Copyright © 2024 by Rachael Reed

Check Out More Great Products and Free Giveaways

https://tbdbpublishing.com/

Chapter 1: Meet the Crew

Alexis stood on the corner, her thin jacket doing little to shield her from the biting cold. The streetlights cast a harsh glow, illuminating the trash-strewn streets and cracked sidewalks. This was her life now—hustling for cash in a city that didn't give a damn about her. She glanced at her phone, the screen cracked, just like her dreams.

"Yo, Lexi, you good?" Jai's voice cut through the night, pulling Alexis from her thoughts. Jai was her ride or die, a girl who'd seen the same rough shit life had thrown her way. Jai, with her dark curls and fierce eyes, had a presence that could make anyone step back. She was tough, no doubt, but there was a vulnerability she tried hard to hide.

"Nah, not really," Alexis muttered, stuffing her hands in her pockets. "This ain't what I thought life would be, ya know?"

Jai nodded, lighting a cigarette. "Ain't none of us thought we'd end up here, but we gotta do what we gotta do. You heard from Rose?"

Alexis shook her head. Rose was the queen bee of their little operation, a veteran escort who'd been in the game longer than they'd been alive. She had connections, money, and the smarts to stay ahead of the cops and the thugs. Rose took them under her wing when they had nowhere else to go, teaching them the rules of the game and how to survive.

"She supposed to be meeting us here," Jai said, exhaling smoke. "Got a big client tonight. Pay good money."

"Good money" was relative. For Alexis and Jai, it meant enough to cover rent, maybe get some decent food, and send a little back home if they were lucky. But it was never enough to escape the life they were trapped in.

Rose rolled up in her sleek black car, the kind that looked out of place in their part of town. She stepped out, exuding confidence and danger. Her hair was perfectly styled, her makeup flawless, her clothes a mix of class and seduction.

"Get in, girls," Rose commanded, not bothering with pleasantries. "We got work to do."

The ride to the club was silent, each of them lost in their thoughts. The club was their domain, a place where they could be whoever the clients wanted them to be. It was dark, loud, and smelled of sweat, alcohol, and desperation. The bouncers nodded at Rose, letting them in without a word.

In the dressing room, Rose handed them their outfits—skimpy, revealing, meant to entice and seduce. "Remember, we're selling a fantasy. Keep it together, no matter what."

Alexis looked at herself in the mirror, trying to see past the makeup and glitter. She was just a girl who'd grown up too fast, who'd seen too much. Her mind drifted to her past—a mother who never cared, a father who disappeared. She had dreams once, of college, a career, but those dreams died a long time ago.

Jai's story wasn't much different. Raised in foster care, bounced from home to home, she learned early on that she could only rely on herself. The streets taught her to be tough, to fight for what she wanted. And what she wanted now was out of this life, but she couldn't see a way out.

Rose watched them, her eyes cold and calculating. She had a past too, but she never talked about it. All they knew was that she was good at what she did, and she expected the same from them.

"Tonight's client is special," Rose said, her voice low. "He's got money, power, and connections. Treat him right, and he'll take care of us."

The night passed in a blur of lights, music, and bodies. Alexis and Jai moved through the crowd, playing their roles perfectly. They smiled, laughed, and flirted, but always kept their guard up. The client, a middle-aged man with a sharp suit and sharper eyes, watched them with interest.

As the night drew to a close, the client made his choice. He wanted both of them. Alexis and Jai exchanged a glance, knowing what was expected of them. They followed him to a private room, their hearts pounding.

The room was luxurious, a stark contrast to the world outside. The client poured drinks, his eyes never leaving them. "You girls are special," he said, his voice smooth. "Rose tells me you're the best."

Alexis forced a smile. "We aim to please."

The client's smile widened, but there was something predatory in his gaze. "Good. Because I have high expectations."

The night turned dark and twisted, the client's demands pushing them to their limits. But they endured, because that's what they were trained to do. When it was over, they stumbled out of the room, exhausted and shaken.

Rose was waiting, her expression unreadable. "You did good," she said, handing them envelopes stuffed with cash. "But remember, this is just the beginning. The game never stops."

As they left the club, Alexis and Jai felt the weight of their lives pressing down on them. They were trapped in a world of shadows and lies, where every day was a fight for survival. But they had each other, and as long as they did, they'd keep playing the game.

Back on the streets, the night was quiet, but danger lurked in every corner. Alexis looked at Jai, her resolve hardening. "We gotta find a way out of this, Jai. We can't do this forever."

Jai nodded, her eyes dark with determination. "We will, Lexi. We just gotta keep our heads up and watch our backs."

As they walked away, the city swallowed them up, two girls lost in a world that didn't care if they lived or died. But they were fighters, and as long as they had breath in their bodies, they'd keep fighting. The game was rigged, but they were determined to beat it, no matter the cost.

Chapter 2: The Hustle Begins

Alexis's breath came out in ragged gasps as she ran through the alley, her heart pounding in her chest. Her hands shook as she clutched the crumpled bills she'd earned tonight. It wasn't enough. It was never enough. She had her little sister, Kayla, waiting at home, hungry and scared. Alexis had to keep hustling, keep grinding, or they'd both be out on the streets.

"Yo, Alexis!" a voice called out. She spun around, eyes wide with fear, but it was just Marcus, one of the local dealers. "You good, girl? Look like you seen a ghost."

Alexis forced a smile. "Just tryin' to get home, Marcus. Ain't no ghosts out here, just real-life monsters."

Marcus laughed, a dark sound that echoed off the walls. "Ain't that the truth. You need anythin', you know where to find me."

Alexis nodded and hurried on, her mind racing. She had to get back to Kayla, make sure she was safe. Their apartment was a rundown, one-bedroom dump, but it was better than nothing. She unlocked the door and slipped inside, finding Kayla asleep on the couch, wrapped in a thin blanket.

Alexis knelt beside her sister, brushing a strand of hair from her face. "I'm sorry, baby girl," she whispered. "I'll get us outta here, I promise."

But promises were easy to make and hard to keep. Alexis knew that better than anyone.

Jai stood outside her apartment, staring at the door. She could hear Tyrone inside, yelling and smashing things. Her body ached from the last beating he'd given her, and she knew she couldn't take much more. She had to get out, had to escape before he killed her.

She took a deep breath and pushed the door open. Tyrone spun around, his eyes bloodshot and wild. "Where the hell you been?" he demanded, advancing on her.

"I went to get us some food," Jai lied, holding up a bag of takeout. "Just tryin' to take care of you."

Tyrone slapped the bag out of her hands, sending food flying. "You think I care 'bout that? You been runnin' around on me, I know it."

Jai backed away, her heart pounding. "I ain't been with nobody but you, Ty. I swear."

He grabbed her by the hair, yanking her close. "You think I'm stupid? You ain't nothin' but a lyin' bitch."

Jai's vision blurred with tears, but she fought to stay calm. "Please, Ty, I love you. I just wanna make things right."

He sneered and shoved her to the floor. "You ain't worth shit. Get outta my sight."

Jai scrambled to her feet and ran, not stopping until she was blocks away. She collapsed on a bench, sobbing. She had nowhere to go, no one to turn to. But then she remembered Rose, the woman she'd met at the club. Rose had offered her a way out, a chance to start over.

With shaking hands, Jai pulled out her phone and dialed Rose's number.

Rose watched Jai pace back and forth in her living room, her eyes red and swollen from crying. "Sit down, Jai. You safe here."

Jai collapsed onto the couch, her body trembling. "Thank you, Rose. I didn't know where else to go."

Rose nodded, her gaze steady. "I told you, I take care of my girls. But you gotta understand, this life ain't easy. It's dangerous and dirty, but it's better than bein' dead."

Jai swallowed hard. "I'll do whatever it takes. I can't go back to Ty."

Rose leaned forward, her expression serious. "This ain't just about shakin' your ass and lookin' pretty. You gotta be smart, gotta know the rules. First rule: never trust nobody. Not even me. Second rule: always get your money up front. No exceptions."

Jai nodded, soaking in every word. "I understand."

Rose continued, her voice cold and clear. "And if you ever feel like you in danger, you call me. I got people who can help. But you gotta be tough, Jai. Ain't no room for weakness in this game."

Alexis glanced nervously around the dimly lit room. She'd heard about Rose from a friend, and now here she was, sitting across from the woman herself. Rose was intimidating, but there was a kindness in her eyes that made Alexis feel a sliver of hope.

"So, you wanna work for me?" Rose asked, her tone blunt.

Alexis nodded. "I need the money. I got a little sister to take care of."

Rose leaned back, studying her. "You know this ain't no walk in the park. It's rough out there, and it ain't gonna get easier."

"I know," Alexis said, her voice firm. "But I ain't got no other choice."

Rose nodded slowly. "Alright, then. You work for me, you follow my rules. You mess up, you on your own. But you do good, and I'll make sure you and your sister are taken care of."

Alexis felt a weight lift off her shoulders. "Thank you, Rose. I won't let you down."

The hustle began that night. Alexis and Jai found themselves thrust into a world they barely understood. The money was good, better than anything they'd ever seen, but the risks were higher. Every night was a gamble, every client a potential threat.

They learned quickly. Rose was a strict teacher, but fair. She taught them how to read people, how to stay safe, how to get what they needed without giving too much. They became a team, watching each other's backs, surviving together.

But the streets were unforgiving. Alexis found herself constantly on edge, worrying about Kayla, about getting caught, about the dangerous men they dealt with. Jai struggled with her own demons, fighting to stay clean, to stay focused.

One night, as they left a high-end club, Rose pulled them aside. "I got a job for you two. Big money, but it's risky. You in?"

Alexis and Jai exchanged a look, their hearts pounding. They knew the stakes, but they also knew they had no other choice.

"We're in," Alexis said, determination in her eyes.

"Good," Rose replied, a sly smile on her lips. "Let's get to work."

As they walked into the night, the city around them buzzed with life. They were just two girls trying to make it in a world that didn't care if they lived or died. But they had each other, and as long as they did, they'd keep fighting.

The game was dangerous, but they were ready. Ready to hustle, ready to survive, ready to play the game, no matter the cost.

Chapter 3: Learning the Ropes

Alexis and Jai sat on Rose's worn-out couch, the dim light casting shadows on their faces. The air was thick with tension and the scent of cheap air freshener. Rose stood before them, her presence commanding and unyielding. She was their mentor now, their guide through the dark and twisted path they had chosen.

"Listen up, girls," Rose began, her voice firm. "This game ain't for the weak. You gotta be sharp, smart, and always one step ahead. Rule number one: never show fear. These clients, they smell fear, they'll eat you alive."

Alexis nodded, her heart racing. She was scared, no doubt, but she knew she had to push through it for Kayla's sake. Jai, sitting next to her, seemed just as tense, her fingers tapping nervously on her knee.

"Rule number two," Rose continued, pacing the room. "Always get your money up front. No exceptions. If a client tries to stiff you, you walk. Ain't no amount of money worth your safety."

Jai looked up, biting her lip. "What if they get aggressive?"

Rose paused, her eyes narrowing. "That's when you call me. I got people who can handle that. But you gotta keep your wits about you, always."

The training sessions were grueling. Rose showed them how to read people, how to gauge a client's intentions from a glance, a touch, a word. They practiced in front of mirrors, learning to perfect their smiles, their allure, their defenses.

"Body language is key," Rose explained one night, as they stood in front of a full-length mirror. "You gotta project confidence, even if you're shaking inside. Stand tall, look 'em in the eye. Make 'em believe you're in control."

Alexis tried to follow Rose's advice, straightening her posture and lifting her chin. She felt ridiculous, but Rose's approving nod gave her a sliver of confidence.

Their first client came sooner than they expected. Rose had arranged everything, and now Alexis and Jai found themselves in a swanky hotel room, the city lights twinkling outside the window. The client, a wealthy businessman with a polished smile and cold eyes, looked them over like they were merchandise.

"Relax," Rose whispered before leaving them alone with the client. "You've got this."

Alexis's heart pounded in her chest as she exchanged a nervous glance with Jai. They were in this together, for better or worse.

The client, Mr. Daniels, poured them drinks, his gaze lingering on them a little too long. "So, how long you been in the business?" he asked, his tone casual but with an edge of curiosity.

Alexis forced a smile, remembering Rose's advice. "Long enough," she replied, her voice steady. "What about you? You been doin' this long?"

Mr. Daniels chuckled, taking a sip of his drink. "Longer than you'd believe."

The night dragged on, a blur of forced smiles and stilted conversation. Alexis and Jai followed Rose's training to the letter, keeping their nerves in check and their smiles plastered on. When it was finally over, Mr. Daniels handed them a thick envelope of cash, his smile as cold as ever.

"Pleasure doing business with you," he said, his tone dismissive.

As soon as he left, Alexis and Jai collapsed on the bed, their bodies trembling from the adrenaline. "We did it," Jai whispered, her voice a mix of relief and exhaustion. "We actually did it."

Alexis nodded, clutching the envelope. "Yeah, we did. But damn, that was tough."

Rose returned, her expression unreadable. "You did good," she said, her tone softer than usual. "You handled yourselves well."

The three women sat in silence for a moment, the weight of what they had just done settling over them. It was the first step in a long and dangerous journey, but they had made it through together.

As the days turned into weeks, Alexis and Jai grew more confident, their bond with Rose deepening. They became a team, a pseudo-family bound by necessity and shared struggle. Rose was more than just their mentor; she was their protector, their guide.

One night, as they sat around Rose's tiny kitchen table, sharing a rare moment of peace, Rose opened up about her own past. "I wasn't always like this," she said, her voice distant. "I had dreams, just like you. But life had other plans."

Alexis listened, her heart aching. "What happened?"

Rose shrugged, a bitter smile on her lips. "Got caught up with the wrong crowd, made some bad choices. Ended up here, just like you. But I learned to survive, to make the best of it."

Jai reached out, squeezing Rose's hand. "We're grateful for everything you've done, Rose. We wouldn't have made it without you."

Rose's eyes softened, a rare moment of vulnerability. "We're in this together, girls. We look out for each other, no matter what."

The bond between them grew stronger with each passing day. They laughed, cried, and fought together, their shared experiences forging an unbreakable connection. They were more than just a team; they were a family.

But the streets were always watching, waiting for a chance to tear them apart. One night, as they returned from a particularly lucrative job, they found their apartment ransacked, everything of value taken. The message was clear: someone was watching, someone who wanted them to know they weren't safe.

Alexis's heart raced as she surveyed the damage, her mind spinning with fear and anger. "Who did this?"

Rose's face was set in a grim line. "I don't know, but we're gonna find out. And when we do, they're gonna regret messin' with us."

Jai looked around, her eyes wide with worry. "What do we do now?"

Rose's gaze was hard, determined. "We stick together. We stay strong. And we show 'em we ain't to be messed with."

As they cleaned up the mess and secured their home, the bond between them only grew stronger. They were a family, and nothing would tear them apart. But the streets were ruthless, and they knew the game was far from over.

With danger lurking around every corner, Alexis, Jai, and Rose steeled themselves for the battles ahead. They had come this far, and they would keep fighting, no matter the cost. The game was brutal, but they were ready to play, ready to win.

And as the night settled around them, they knew one thing for sure: they had each other, and that was enough to face whatever the streets threw their way.

Chapter 4: Tensions Rise

Alexis paced the small living room, her mind racing with anger and fear. Rose sat across from her, arms crossed, her face a mask of stern resolve. The air was thick with tension, the kind that made the hairs on the back of your neck stand up.

"This shit's gettin' too dangerous, Rose," Alexis said, her voice sharp. "We almost got caught last night. Cops were everywhere."

Rose's eyes narrowed. "That's the game, Alexis. You knew what you were signin' up for. We gotta stay sharp, keep our heads down."

Alexis stopped pacing, turning to face Rose. "I got a little sister to think about. If I get locked up, who's gonna take care of her? We need to find a safer way."

Rose stood, her presence towering. "There ain't no safe way in this life. You want out, you walk now. But you walk alone. We in this together, or not at all."

The words hung in the air, heavy and unforgiving. Alexis's fists clenched at her sides, her heart pounding. She knew Rose was right, but the fear gnawed at her, threatening to consume her.

Jai stumbled into the apartment, her eyes glazed, a dreamy smile on her lips. Alexis and Rose turned to her, their expressions shifting from anger to concern. Jai's walk was unsteady, her movements slow and deliberate.

"Jai, what the hell?" Alexis demanded, rushing to her side. "You been usin'?"

Jai giggled, swaying slightly. "Just a lil' somethin' to take the edge off. Ain't no big deal."

Rose's face darkened, her voice a low growl. "What you usin', Jai? You know that shit'll mess you up."

Jai's smile faded, replaced by a stubborn glare. "I ain't a child, Rose. I can handle it."

Rose stepped forward, grabbing Jai by the shoulders. "No, you can't. That shit'll ruin you. You think you can play with fire and not get burned?"

Jai pushed her away, her eyes flashing with anger. "I ain't you, Rose. I can control it. Just needed a break, that's all."

Alexis watched, her heart aching. She knew the dangers of the streets, the temptations that lurked around every corner. She stepped between them, trying to diffuse the situation. "We gotta stick together. Can't afford to be fightin' each other."

Rose's gaze shifted to Alexis, her anger still simmering. "Tell that to her. She needs to get her head straight."

Jai stormed out of the room, slamming the door behind her. The silence that followed was deafening, each of them lost in their own thoughts and fears.

The streets were unforgiving, a constant reminder of the harsh realities they faced. Every corner held a new danger, every alley a potential trap. Alexis felt the weight of it all pressing down on her, the fear, the uncertainty, the constant struggle to survive.

One night, as they walked the darkened streets, a group of men approached, their intentions clear. Rose stepped forward, her stance protective. "We don't want no trouble."

The leader of the group, a tall, muscular man with a sneer on his face, laughed. "Too late for that, sweetheart. You in our territory now."

Alexis's heart pounded as she glanced at Jai, who seemed more distracted than usual. The men closed in, their eyes predatory. Alexis's mind raced, searching for a way out.

Rose's voice cut through the tension. "Back off. We ain't lookin' for a fight."

The leader's sneer widened. "Too bad. We are."

Before they could react, the men lunged, fists flying. Alexis ducked, her instincts kicking in. She fought back, her fear fueling her strength. Rose was a whirlwind of movement, her years of experience evident in every punch and kick. Jai, however, seemed slow, her reactions dulled by whatever she had taken.

The fight was brutal, the sound of flesh hitting flesh echoing through the night. Alexis's vision blurred, blood dripping from a cut above her eye. She fought with everything she had, knowing that giving up wasn't an option.

Finally, the men retreated, nursing their wounds. Rose stood tall, her breathing heavy, her eyes blazing with fury. Alexis staggered, her body aching, her mind racing. Jai leaned against a wall, her face pale, her eyes unfocused.

"We gotta be smarter," Rose said, her voice hoarse. "Can't let our guard down."

Alexis nodded, wiping the blood from her face. "We can't keep doin' this. Somethin' gotta change."

Rose's gaze softened slightly. "I know. But we gotta stick together, stay strong."

Back at the apartment, they tended to their wounds in silence. The fight had shaken them, a stark reminder of the dangers they faced every day. Alexis watched Jai, her heart heavy with worry. Jai was slipping, the lure of drugs pulling her deeper into darkness.

"Jai, you gotta stop," Alexis said softly, her voice pleading. "That shit's gonna kill you."

Jai looked up, tears in her eyes. "I know. But it's hard, Lexi. It helps me forget, just for a little while."

Alexis reached out, squeezing her hand. "We in this together. We gotta look out for each other."

Jai nodded, her expression filled with regret. "I'll try. I promise."

Rose entered the room, her presence a comforting strength. "We get through this together. No more fights, no more distractions. We focus on the job, on each other."

The three women sat in silence, the weight of their decisions pressing down on them. They were a family, bound by necessity and shared struggle. But the streets were unforgiving, and they knew the game was far from over.

The days that followed were a blur of tension and unease. Alexis and Jai tried to stay focused, but the constant threat of danger loomed over them. They moved through the city like shadows, always watching, always waiting.

One night, as they prepared for another job, Alexis felt a chill run down her spine. Something didn't feel right. She glanced at Rose, who seemed more tense than usual.

"Rose, you okay?" Alexis asked, her voice low.

Rose's eyes were hard, her jaw set. "Just got a bad feeling, that's all. We gotta be careful."

As they stepped out into the night, Alexis couldn't shake the feeling that they were being watched. The city was alive with danger, and they were just pawns in a game they couldn't control.

The hustle never stopped; the dangers never ceased. But they were fighters, survivors. And as long as they had each other, they would keep playing the game, no matter the cost. The streets were ruthless, but they were ready to face whatever came their way.

The night was dark, the air thick with tension. They walked into the unknown, their hearts pounding, their minds racing. The game was on, and there was no turning back.

Chapter 5: Betrayal

Alexis sat on the edge of her bed, staring at the crack in the ceiling. Something wasn't right. Rose had been acting strange lately, making secret phone calls, stepping out without explaining where she was going. Alexis's gut told her that Rose was hiding something, and in their line of work, secrets could be deadly.

"Yo, Lexi, you good?" Jai's voice slurred from the bathroom. Alexis sighed, knowing Jai was high again. It was becoming a daily thing, and it was tearing them apart.

Alexis stood up, walking to the bathroom door. "Jai, we need to talk. This shit you doin', it ain't safe. You gonna get yourself killed."

Jai emerged, her eyes glassy, her movements slow. "I can handle it, Lexi. Just need it to take the edge off."

Alexis shook her head, frustration boiling over. "No, you can't. You think you can keep usin' and not get caught up? You messin' with your life, and mine too."

Jai stumbled, grabbing onto the sink for support. "I'm sorry, Lexi. I just... I can't deal with all this. It's too much."

Alexis took a deep breath, trying to keep her cool. "We in this together, Jai. But you gotta get clean. We can't afford no mistakes."

Jai nodded, tears welling in her eyes. "I'll try. I promise."

The tension in the apartment was palpable. Alexis's suspicion about Rose grew stronger every day. She decided to confront Rose, but she had to be careful. Rose was sharp, and if she felt cornered, it could turn ugly.

One night, after a long day of hustling, Alexis waited for Rose to come home. The door creaked open, and Rose stepped inside, looking worn out but alert.

"Rose, we need to talk," Alexis said, her voice steady.

Rose raised an eyebrow, closing the door behind her. "What's on your mind, Alexis?"

Alexis took a deep breath, her heart pounding. "I know you been hidin' somethin'. You makin' calls, disappearin'. What's goin' on?"

Rose's eyes hardened, her expression unreadable. "You don't trust me?"

Alexis crossed her arms, standing her ground. "It ain't about trust. It's about survival. If you hidin' somethin', it puts us all at risk."

Rose sighed, her shoulders slumping slightly. "I'm tryin' to protect you, Alexis. There's things you don't need to know. Just trust me on this."

Alexis shook her head, frustration bubbling up. "How can I trust you if you keepin' secrets? We supposed to be a team, Rose."

Rose's gaze softened, but there was a hardness beneath it. "I do what I gotta do to keep us safe. You don't like it, you can walk. But don't you dare question my loyalty."

Alexis bit back her retort, knowing she wouldn't get any more answers tonight. She turned away, her mind racing with doubt and fear.

Jai's addiction was spiraling out of control. Alexis found her passed out in the bathroom more than once, her eyes vacant, her body frail. The friction between them grew, their once strong bond now frayed and fragile.

"Jai, you gotta get clean," Alexis pleaded one night, her voice breaking. "You gonna get us all killed."

Jai looked up, her eyes filled with tears. "I know, Lexi. I just... I can't stop. It hurts too much."

Alexis knelt beside her, taking her hand. "We in this together. We can get through this, but you gotta fight. You gotta want it."

Jai nodded, her grip weak. "I'll try, Lexi. For you."

One night, as they were preparing for a job, Rose received a call. Her face turned pale, and she quickly ended the call, her hands trembling. Alexis's suspicion flared up again.

"Who was that?" Alexis asked, trying to keep her voice casual.

Rose glanced at her, her eyes guarded. "Just an old client. Nothin' to worry about."

But Alexis wasn't convinced. Something about the way Rose reacted set off alarm bells in her mind. She decided to keep a close eye on Rose, ready for anything.

Later that week, they met with a client named Victor, one of Rose's old contacts. He was slick, dressed in a tailored suit, but there was something off about him. His eyes were cold, predatory.

"Good to see you, Rose," Victor said, his voice smooth as silk. "These must be your new girls."

Rose nodded, her expression tense. "This is Alexis and Jai. They're good at what they do."

Victor's gaze lingered on Alexis, making her skin crawl. "I bet they are."

The night proceeded as usual, but Alexis couldn't shake the feeling that something was wrong. Victor was too interested, too familiar. She kept a close watch, her instincts on high alert.

As the night wound down, Victor cornered Rose, his voice low and menacing. "You owe me, Rose. And I'm here to collect."

Rose's face paled, her eyes wide with fear. "Victor, I told you, I need more time."

Victor sneered, grabbing Rose by the arm. "Time's up. You either pay up, or I take what's mine."

Alexis's heart pounded as she watched the confrontation. She stepped forward, ready to intervene. "Let her go."

Victor's eyes flicked to Alexis, his expression cold. "Stay out of this, little girl. This is between me and Rose."

Rose struggled, her voice shaking. "Alexis, stay back. I can handle this."

But Alexis couldn't stand by and do nothing. She lunged forward, trying to pull Victor away from Rose. The room erupted into chaos, fists flying, bodies crashing into furniture.

Jai, still groggy from her latest high, stumbled into the room, her eyes wide with confusion. "What's goin' on?"

Victor's men burst into the apartment, weapons drawn. Alexis's blood ran cold as she realized they were outnumbered, outgunned. She fought desperately, but it was no use.

Victor's men grabbed Alexis and Jai, holding them at gunpoint. Victor turned to Rose, his expression triumphant. "You had your chance, Rose. Now, you pay the price."

Rose's eyes filled with tears, her voice breaking. "Please, Victor. Don't hurt them. I'll do anything."

Victor smiled, a cold, cruel smile. "Too late for that. You're mine now."

As the men dragged them away, Alexis's mind raced, fear and anger mixing into a deadly cocktail. She knew they were in deep trouble, and the only way out was to fight with everything they had.

The night was dark, the air thick with danger. Alexis, Jai, and Rose were caught in a deadly game, and the stakes had never been higher. They had to stay strong, stay united, and find a way to survive. The streets were ruthless, but they were ready to face whatever came their way.

And as they were thrown into the back of a van, Alexis vowed to herself that she would find a way to protect her sister, her friends, and herself. No matter the cost.

Chapter 6: A New Player

The night was thick with tension as Alexis and Jai walked down the dimly lit street. The neon lights from the strip clubs and bars cast an eerie glow, highlighting the rough edges of the city. The buzz of the streets was ever-present, a constant reminder of the life they were entrenched in. Tonight felt different, though. Something was in the air, a change, a shift.

"Yo, Alexis, you feel that?" Jai asked, her voice low, eyes darting around. "Somethin' ain't right."

Alexis nodded, her senses on high alert. They turned the corner and spotted a sleek black car idling at the curb. The door opened, and out stepped Marcus, a tall, smooth-talking pimp with a reputation that preceded him. His suit was sharp, his smile even sharper.

"Ladies," Marcus greeted, his voice smooth as silk. "I been hearin' about y'all. Rose's girls, right?"

Alexis exchanged a wary glance with Jai. "Who's askin'?"

Marcus chuckled, taking a step closer. "Name's Marcus. I run things around here, make sure my girls are taken care of. And I gotta say, I'm impressed with y'all. Rose been holdin' y'all back."

Jai's eyes flickered with curiosity. "What you mean, holdin' us back?"

Marcus's smile widened. "You got potential, but Rose, she's old news. I can take y'all places, get you the kinda money you only dream about. Real safety, real security."

Alexis felt a pang of doubt. Marcus's words were like honey, sweet but sticky. "We good with Rose. She take care of us."

Marcus's gaze hardened, his charm never wavering. "Is that right? From what I hear, Rose's been slippin'. Y'all deserve better. Deserve more."

Over the next few days, Marcus kept popping up, always with that same smooth talk, always with promises of a better life. Alexis tried to ignore him, tried to stay focused, but his words lingered in her mind, gnawing at her loyalty to Rose.

One night, as they were wrapping up a job, Marcus appeared again. This time, he was more direct, more insistent. "Alexis, Jai, y'all need to think about your futures. Rose can't offer you what I can. I got connections, money, power. Everything you need to get outta this grind."

Jai seemed to be wavering, her eyes reflecting the temptation. "Maybe he's right, Lexi. Maybe we need to think 'bout ourselves for once."

Alexis's heart pounded. She couldn't deny the allure of Marcus's promises, but something about him felt off, dangerous. "I dunno, Jai. Rose been good to us. We can't just ditch her."

Marcus stepped closer, his voice dropping to a conspiratorial whisper. "Rose don't need to know. Y'all can work for me on the side, see how it feels. No harm in tryin'."

Jai looked at Alexis, her expression pleading. "Just think about it, Lexi. We ain't gotta decide now."

That night, Alexis lay in bed, staring at the ceiling. Her mind was a whirlwind of confusion and doubt. Rose had taken them in, taught them everything they knew. But Marcus's words echoed in her head. Was Rose really holding them back? Could they have a better life with Marcus?

She turned to Jai, who was already drifting off to sleep. "Jai, you really think we should go with Marcus?"

Jai sighed, turning to face Alexis. "I don't know, Lexi. But I'm tired of this. Tired of strugglin', tired of feelin' scared all the time. Maybe he can help us."

Alexis's heart ached. She didn't want to betray Rose, but the thought of a better life was hard to ignore. "We gotta be careful. Marcus ain't tellin' us everything. We need to know what we gettin' into."

The next day, Alexis and Jai met with Marcus again, this time in a more private setting. He laid out his plan, painting a picture of a life filled with luxury and safety. But Alexis couldn't shake the feeling that it was all too good to be true.

"So, what y'all think?" Marcus asked, leaning back in his chair, exuding confidence.

Alexis took a deep breath, her mind racing. "We need time to think, Marcus. This ain't a decision we can make overnight."

Marcus nodded, his smile never fading. "Take all the time you need. Just know, I ain't gonna wait forever. Opportunities like this don't come 'round often."

As they left, Alexis's mind was a tangled mess of loyalty and temptation. She couldn't deny the appeal of Marcus's offer, but the thought of betraying Rose felt like a knife in her gut. She needed to talk to Rose, needed to understand what was really going on.

That evening, Alexis found Rose alone, her expression tired but resilient. "Rose, we need to talk."

Rose looked up, sensing the gravity in Alexis's tone. "What's on your mind?"

Alexis took a deep breath, her hands trembling. "Marcus's been talkin' to us. He say you holdin' us back, that he can give us a better life."

Rose's eyes darkened, a mix of hurt and anger flashing across her face. "Marcus is a snake, Alexis. He's all about control, about using people for his own gain. Don't let him fool you."

Alexis felt torn, her loyalty to Rose battling with the lure of Marcus's promises. "But what if he's right? What if we could have more, be safer?"

Rose stood, her gaze fierce. "Safety with Marcus comes at a price. You think he cares about y'all? He sees you as commodities, not people. I took you in, not for what you could give me, but because I saw potential, saw two girls who needed a chance."

Alexis's heart ached with the weight of Rose's words. She wanted to believe Rose, wanted to trust her. But the doubt lingered, a poison seeping into her thoughts.

That night, Alexis couldn't sleep. She replayed the conversations over and over, her mind a battleground of conflicting emotions. She knew she had to make a decision, one that would change everything.

In the early hours of the morning, she got up, her heart pounding. She found Jai awake, staring out the window, lost in her own thoughts.

"Jai, we need to decide. We can't keep goin' back and forth."

Jai turned to her, her eyes filled with uncertainty. "I know, Lexi. But I don't know what to do."

Alexis took a deep breath, her voice steady. "We gotta trust our instincts. Marcus might offer us more, but at what cost? Rose's been there for us, taught us how to survive. We can't just throw that away."

Jai nodded slowly, the tension in her shoulders easing. "You right, Lexi. We stick with Rose. We figure out a way to make it work."

As the first light of dawn crept through the window, Alexis felt a sense of resolve. They would stay with Rose, fight to make their own way. The streets were ruthless, but they had each other. And that, she hoped, would be enough to see them through.

The decision made, they knew the road ahead would be tough. But they were ready to face whatever came their way, together. The game was far from over, and they were determined to play it on their own terms.

Chapter 7: The Fall

The tension in the apartment was thick enough to cut with a knife. Jai had been spending more and more time with Marcus, and Alexis could see the change in her. She was drawn to his smooth talk, his promises of a better life, and it was driving a wedge between her and Alexis.

"Jai, we need to talk," Alexis said, trying to keep her voice steady.

Jai barely looked up from her phone. "What about, Lexi?"

Alexis felt her frustration boiling over. "About you and Marcus. You know he ain't good for you."

Jai sighed, finally meeting Alexis's eyes. "Marcus cares about me. He's given me more in these few weeks than we ever had with Rose."

"That's bullshit, Jai, and you know it," Alexis snapped. "Rose took us in, taught us everything. Marcus just sees you as another piece to his puzzle."

Jai stood, her face flushed with anger. "You just jealous 'cause he picked me and not you. Maybe you the one who's scared of a better life."

Alexis's heart pounded, a mix of anger and hurt. "This ain't about jealousy. It's about loyalty. Rose been there for us, and you throwin' it all away for some pimp."

Jai's eyes flashed with defiance. "I'm done with this. I'm done with you, and I'm done with Rose. Marcus is my future, and I'm takin' it."

With that, Jai stormed out, leaving Alexis alone with her thoughts and the heavy silence of betrayal.

Jai's new life with Marcus was far from the glamorous escape she had imagined. The promises of safety and luxury quickly evaporated, replaced by the harsh reality of control and manipulation. Marcus's charm was a mask, hiding the darkness beneath.

Jai found herself in dangerous situations, dealing with clients who were rough and demanding. The money was good, but the cost was high. Every night, she returned to Marcus's place with new bruises and a heavier heart.

One night, Marcus's true nature revealed itself. Jai had just finished a particularly rough job when Marcus cornered her, his eyes cold and calculating. "You ain't makin' enough, Jai. I need you to step it up."

Jai's heart raced with fear. "I'm doin' my best, Marcus. Some of these clients... they're too much."

Marcus grabbed her by the arm, his grip tight and painful. "You think I care? You in this to make money, my money. You better start earnin' your keep."

Jai nodded, tears welling in her eyes. "I'll do better, I promise."

Marcus released her, a cruel smile on his lips. "Good. Don't disappoint me."

Back at the apartment, Rose could sense the growing danger. She saw the changes in Jai, the signs of abuse and control. She knew Marcus was bad news, and she couldn't just stand by and watch Jai destroy herself.

One night, Rose decided to confront Marcus. She found him at one of his usual haunts, a dimly lit bar filled with shady characters. She approached him, her expression fierce and determined.

"Marcus, we need to talk," Rose said, her voice steady despite the fear gnawing at her insides.

Marcus looked up, his eyes narrowing. "Rose. What brings you here?"

"Jai," Rose replied, not backing down. "You need to let her go. She ain't built for this life, and you know it."

Marcus chuckled, a dark sound that sent chills down Rose's spine. "Jai's mine now. She made her choice."

Rose leaned in, her eyes blazing with anger. "You don't own her, Marcus. She's more than just a pawn in your game."

Marcus's smile faded, his expression turning deadly. "You better watch yourself, Rose. You don't want to start a war you can't win."

Rose stood her ground, refusing to be intimidated. "This ain't over, Marcus. I'll get her back, no matter what it takes."

Jai's situation grew worse with each passing day. Marcus's demands became more brutal, and the clients more dangerous. She felt trapped, her dreams of a better life crumbling around her. She thought about Alexis and Rose, the life she had left behind. She realized too late that she had traded one hell for another.

One night, after a particularly violent encounter, Jai found herself alone in a dingy hotel room, her body aching, her spirit broken. She pulled out her phone and stared at the screen, her fingers hovering over Alexis's number.

She finally dialed, her heart pounding. "Alexis, it's me."

Alexis's voice on the other end was a mix of relief and anger. "Jai, where the hell have you been? I've been worried sick."

"I'm sorry, Lexi," Jai whispered, tears streaming down her face. "I made a mistake. I need your help."

The reunion was tense, filled with unspoken words and heavy emotions. Alexis and Rose welcomed Jai back, but the damage was done. The trust had been shattered, and the path to healing was long and uncertain.

Rose took Jai's hand, her voice soft but firm. "We're here for you, Jai. But you gotta promise me, no more Marcus."

Jai nodded, her eyes filled with remorse. "I promise, Rose. I'm done with him. I just want to make things right."

As they sat together, the weight of their choices pressing down on them, they knew the road ahead would be tough. The streets were ruthless, and the dangers were ever-present. But they were a family, bound by loyalty and love. And as long as they had each other, they would find a way to survive.

That night, as they lay in their beds, the city outside buzzing with life, Alexis felt a glimmer of hope. They had been through hell, but they had come out the other side, bruised but not broken. The game was far from over, and the stakes were higher than ever. But they were ready to face whatever came their way, together.

The streets were dark, the future uncertain. But they had each other, and that was enough. For now.

Chapter 8: The Setup

The night was humid and oppressive, a storm brewing in the distance. Rose, Alexis, and Jai sat around the small kitchen table, the tension palpable. Jai was still recovering from her ordeal with Marcus, and the trust between the three was fragile.

"We gotta stay low for a while," Rose said, her voice steady but her eyes betraying her worry. "Marcus ain't gonna take kindly to Jai leavin.'"

Alexis nodded, her jaw clenched. "He ain't gonna just let it go. We need to be ready for whatever he throws at us."

The knock at the door was sharp, unexpected. Rose exchanged a wary glance with Alexis and got up to answer it. The moment she opened the door, chaos erupted. Police officers stormed in, shouting orders, guns drawn. Rose was tackled to the ground, her face pressed against the cold, dirty floor.

"Get down! Hands behind your back!" an officer shouted, yanking Alexis to her feet and slapping handcuffs on her wrists.

Jai screamed, trying to run, but was quickly subdued. The apartment was torn apart, the officers searching for evidence. Rose's mind raced, realizing this was a setup. Marcus had tipped off the cops to eliminate her, take her out of the game.

"You got the wrong people!" Rose yelled, struggling against the officer's grip. "We ain't done nothin'!"

The officer sneered. "Save it for the judge."

The jail was a cold, unforgiving place, the walls echoing with the sounds of despair. Alexis and Rose were separated, each thrown into a small, cramped cell. The reality of their situation hit Alexis hard as she sat on the thin mattress, staring at the barred window.

"Yo, new girl, what you in for?" a rough voice called from across the cell block.

Alexis looked up, her eyes adjusting to the dim light. "Got set up. Ain't done nothin' wrong."

The other woman laughed, a harsh, bitter sound. "Yeah, that's what they all say. Welcome to hell."

Days turned into weeks, the monotonous routine of prison life wearing them down. The guards were cruel, the other inmates even crueler. Rose, a veteran of the streets, held her own, but Alexis struggled, her spirit slowly being crushed by the grim reality of their situation.

One night, as the lights flickered out, Alexis lay on her bunk, her mind racing. She missed Kayla, worried about what would happen to her sister now. She thought of Jai, of Rose, and the betrayal that had led them here. She knew they had to find a way out, had to fight back.

"Rose," Alexis whispered through the bars separating their cells. "We gotta do somethin'. We can't rot in here."

Rose's voice was steady but filled with resolve. "I know. We gotta keep our heads down, play it smart. We get our day in court, we prove we were set up."

Alexis sighed, the weight of their situation pressing down on her. "I just... I can't stand bein' in here. It's like a nightmare."

Rose's eyes softened, a rare moment of vulnerability. "We survive, Alexis. That's what we do. We survive, and then we get even."

The days dragged on, each one blending into the next. The food was barely edible, the cells were cold and damp, and the guards seemed to delight in making their lives miserable. Alexis learned quickly to keep her head down, avoid trouble, and wait for the moment she could strike back.

One afternoon, as she sat in the yard, a familiar figure approached. It was Jai, looking worn and defeated. She had managed to stay out of jail, but the guilt and fear were written all over her face.

"Alexis," Jai whispered, her eyes darting around nervously. "I'm so sorry. This is all my fault."

Alexis stood, her anger bubbling up. "Yeah, it is. But we ain't got time for blame. We need to figure out how to get outta here."

Jai nodded, tears streaming down her face. "I'll do whatever it takes. I swear."

Rose joined them, her presence a calming force. "We need to find a way to prove we were set up. Jai, you need to gather any evidence you can find. We got one shot at this."

The courtroom was intimidating, the judge's gavel echoing like a death knell. Rose and Alexis stood side by side, their chains clinking with every movement. The prosecutor painted them as hardened criminals, manipulating the system for their gain. But they knew the truth, and they were determined to fight.

Jai sat in the back, her eyes wide with fear but her heart filled with resolve. She had managed to gather some evidence, but it was a long shot. The trial was a blur of testimonies and arguments, each side trying to sway the jury.

As the days passed, the tension grew. The prosecutor was relentless, but Rose and Alexis held their ground. They told their story, of how Marcus had set them up, how they were just trying to survive.

The night before the verdict, Alexis lay awake, her mind racing. She thought of Kayla, of the life she had hoped to build. She knew the odds were against them, but she couldn't give up. She wouldn't give up.

The next morning, the jury filed in, their expressions unreadable. The judge asked for the verdict, and time seemed to stand still.

"Not guilty," the foreman said, and Alexis felt a wave of relief wash over her. Tears streamed down her face as she turned to Rose, who nodded, a rare smile on her lips.

As they walked out of the courtroom, free but changed, Alexis knew their fight wasn't over. Marcus was still out there, a threat that loomed large. But they were stronger now, more determined than ever.

The streets were still dangerous, the game still brutal. But they had each other, and that was enough. For now, they were free, and they would fight to stay that way.

The night was dark, the future uncertain. But they had survived, and that was a start. They walked into the unknown, their hearts filled with resolve. The game was far from over, and they were ready to play it on their own terms.

Chapter 9: Jailhouse Politics

The steel doors clanged shut behind Rose and Alexis, sealing them into a world of concrete and iron. The echoes of the door reverberated through the cold, lifeless hallways of the prison, a constant reminder of their grim reality. Alexis glanced at Rose, who remained stoic and resolute. They had survived the streets, but prison was a different beast altogether.

"Keep ya head down and don't trust nobody," Rose whispered as they were led to their cells. "We gotta navigate this shit smart."

Alexis nodded, trying to suppress the fear gnawing at her insides. The cells were small, the air thick with the stench of sweat and despair. As the doors clanged shut behind them, she realized just how alone they were in this place.

The first few days were a blur of harsh realities. The guards were indifferent at best, brutal at worst. The other inmates eyed them warily, sizing them up. Survival here meant more than just staying alive; it meant forming alliances, making connections, finding strength in numbers.

"Yo, Rose," a voice called from across the yard one day. A tall, muscular woman with a shaved head approached them. "Heard you from the streets. Name's Big Dee. We run this block."

Rose nodded, her gaze steady. "Rose. This here's Alexis. We just tryin' to survive."

Big Dee sized them up, then smiled. "Aight. You roll with us, we got your back. But you gotta pull your weight."

Alexis felt a wave of relief. Big Dee's crew was known for being tough but fair. Aligning with them meant protection, a chance to navigate the treacherous waters of prison life.

Days turned into weeks, and Alexis and Rose settled into a grim routine. They kept their heads down, worked their assigned jobs, and stayed out of trouble. But the threat of violence was always present, lurking in the shadows.

One afternoon, as they sat in the yard, Rose leaned in close to Alexis. "We can't just survive, Lexi. We gotta get even. Marcus set us up, and we can't let that slide."

Alexis's heart raced. "What you got in mind?"

Rose's eyes blazed with determination. "We start plannin'. We get outta here, we take him down."

The prison was a world of its own, with its own rules and power dynamics. Rose and Alexis knew they had to play the game if they wanted to survive and exact their revenge. They formed bonds with other inmates, trading favors and gathering information.

"Yo, Lexi," Big Dee called one day. "Got some intel for you. Marcus been makin' moves on the outside. He think he got y'all out the way for good."

Alexis's blood boiled. "We gotta stop him, Dee. He's a snake."

Big Dee nodded. "We got connections. We can get messages out, get people workin' on the outside."

Rose leaned in, her voice low and conspiratorial. "We need to gather evidence, prove he set us up. We get that, we got leverage."

The plan was risky, but they had no choice. They couldn't just sit and rot while Marcus continued his reign. They started small, sending messages through trusted contacts, gathering intel bit by bit.

One night, as they sat in their cell, Rose turned to Alexis, her expression serious. "We gotta stay sharp, Lexi. This place can break you if you let it. We can't lose sight of what we fightin' for."

Alexis nodded, determination hardening her resolve. "We won't, Rose. We get outta here, we take Marcus down. We make him pay."

The days were long, the nights even longer. They faced constant threats, from both inmates and guards. But their alliance with Big Dee's crew provided a semblance of security. They watched each other's backs, shared what little they had, and stayed focused on their goal.

One day, as they were working in the laundry room, a fight broke out between two rival gangs. The room erupted into chaos, fists flying, bodies crashing into machinery. Alexis and Rose ducked and dodged, trying to stay out of the fray.

"Stay low!" Rose shouted, grabbing Alexis and pulling her behind a row of washing machines.

The guards stormed in, batons swinging, breaking up the fight with brutal efficiency. Alexis's heart pounded as she watched the carnage, a stark reminder of the constant danger they faced.

Later, as they returned to their cells, Rose's mind was racing. "We gotta speed up our plans, Lexi. We ain't got time to waste."

Alexis nodded, her resolve hardening. "We do whatever it takes, Rose. We get outta here, we get even."

The prison grapevine was alive with rumors and whispers. Rose and Alexis listened carefully, piecing together information, formulating their strategy. They knew they had to be smart, had to be patient. But the time for action was drawing near.

One evening, Big Dee approached them, her expression serious. "Got a message from the outside. Your girl Jai been workin' on gatherin' evidence. She got people helpin' her."

Rose's eyes lit up with hope. "That's good news. We need all the help we can get."

Big Dee nodded. "Keep your heads down, stay strong. We got your back."

The tension in the prison was palpable, the air thick with anticipation. Rose and Alexis knew the risks, but they also knew they couldn't let Marcus get away with what he'd done. They had to stay focused, had to keep pushing forward.

One night, as they lay in their bunks, Rose whispered through the darkness. "We get outta here, we take Marcus down, we get our lives back."

Alexis nodded, her voice filled with determination. "We will, Rose. We ain't gonna let him win."

The days grew longer, the nights colder. But Rose and Alexis were united in their purpose, their bond forged in the fires of adversity. They were survivors, fighters, and they would not be broken.

As they navigated the treacherous waters of prison life, they kept their eyes on the prize. They knew the path ahead was fraught with danger, but they were ready. They would fight, they would survive, and they would get their revenge.

The game was far from over, and they were ready to play it on their own terms. The streets were ruthless, but so were they. And as long as they had each other, they would find a way to win. The night was dark, the future uncertain, but their resolve was unshakable. They would rise, they would fight, and they would reclaim their lives.

Chapter 10: Jai's Downward Spiral

Jai sat on the edge of the bed, her body aching from the night before. Marcus had shown his true colors, and they were dark, twisted shades of cruelty. The bruises on her arms and the cut on her lip were reminders of his rage, his fists, and his twisted version of love.

"Get up," Marcus barked from the doorway, his eyes cold and devoid of any warmth. "We got clients waitin'. Ain't no time for rest."

Jai winced as she stood, her body protesting every movement. "I can't keep doin' this, Marcus. You promised it wouldn't be like this."

Marcus sneered, stepping closer until his breath was hot on her face. "Promises don't mean shit in this world, Jai. You either do what I say, or you find yourself out on the street with nothin'."

Tears welled up in Jai's eyes, but she blinked them away. She couldn't show weakness, not to him. "I just need a break, that's all. Just a lil' time to heal."

Marcus grabbed her chin, forcing her to look at him. "Ain't no breaks in this game, girl. You belong to me now. You better get used to it."

Jai nodded, her heart breaking. She felt trapped, isolated from the world she once knew. She had made a terrible mistake, and now she was paying the price.

The days blurred together, each one a repeat of the last. Jai found herself spiraling deeper into despair, her only solace the brief moments she could steal away to think of a way out. The drugs helped numb the pain, but they also clouded her mind, making it harder to see a clear path forward.

One night, after a particularly brutal encounter with a client, Jai lay in the dark, her mind racing. She knew she couldn't go on like this. She had to find a way out, had to reach out to someone who could help her. She thought of Alexis and Rose, the family she had turned her back on. They were her only hope.

With trembling hands, she picked up her phone and dialed Alexis's number. The phone rang and rang, and just as she was about to give up, Alexis answered.

"Jai? Is that you?" Alexis's voice was a mix of relief and anger.

"Lexi, I... I need help," Jai whispered, her voice cracking. "I made a mistake. Marcus... he's not who I thought he was. I can't do this anymore."

Alexis's voice softened, concern evident in her tone. "Where are you, Jai? We need to get you outta there."

Jai's eyes filled with tears. "I don't know how, Lexi. I'm trapped. He won't let me go."

"We'll find a way," Alexis said, determination in her voice. "Just hold on, Jai. We'll get you out."

The next few days were a blur of fear and desperation. Jai tried to keep a low profile, avoiding Marcus's wrath as best she could. She knew Alexis and Rose were working on a plan, but every moment spent in Marcus's clutches felt like an eternity.

One evening, Marcus stormed into the room, his eyes blazing with anger. "You been talkin' to someone, ain't you? I can tell."

Jai's heart raced, her mind scrambling for an excuse. "No, Marcus, I ain't talked to nobody. You know I wouldn't do that."

Marcus grabbed her by the throat, his grip tightening. "Don't lie to me, Jai. I ain't stupid. You think you can play me?"

Jai struggled to breathe, her vision blurring. "I'm sorry, Marcus. Please, don't."

He threw her to the ground, his face twisted in rage. "You better watch yourself, girl. Next time you even think 'bout crossin' me, you won't be so lucky."

Jai lay on the floor, gasping for air, tears streaming down her face. She knew she had to get out, and soon. Marcus was becoming more unstable, more dangerous with each passing day.

That night, Jai managed to sneak away to a quiet corner of the house. She dialed Alexis's number again, her hands shaking.

"Lexi, it's getting worse," Jai whispered, her voice trembling. "I don't know how much more I can take."

"We're close, Jai," Alexis said, her voice filled with determination. "We got a plan. Just hang on a little longer."

Jai nodded, trying to hold on to the sliver of hope Alexis offered. "I trust you, Lexi. Please, hurry."

The plan was risky, but it was all they had. Rose and Alexis had managed to gather enough evidence to expose Marcus's operations. They just needed to get Jai out safely.

One night, while Marcus was out, Jai packed a small bag with essentials. Her heart pounded as she made her way to the back door, praying she wouldn't be caught. She slipped out into the night, the cool air a stark contrast to the oppressive heat of Marcus's control.

She met Alexis and Rose at a designated spot, her heart pounding with both fear and relief. Alexis hugged her tightly, her eyes filled with tears. "We got you, Jai. You're safe now."

Rose stepped forward, her expression serious. "We ain't outta the woods yet. We gotta move fast."

They drove through the night, heading to a safe house where they could lay low and plan their next move. Jai felt a mixture of fear and relief, knowing she was finally free from Marcus but also aware of the dangers that still lurked.

As they settled into the safe house, Rose laid out their plan. "We got enough evidence to take Marcus down. But we gotta be smart about it. He's dangerous, and he won't go down easy."

Jai nodded, her resolve hardening. "I'm ready. I ain't gonna let him control me no more."

Alexis squeezed her hand, her eyes filled with determination. "We're in this together, Jai. We take him down, we get our lives back."

The nights were long and filled with planning. They knew Marcus would come looking for Jai, and they had to be ready. But for the first time in a long while, Jai felt a glimmer of hope. She wasn't alone anymore.

She had Alexis and Rose, and together, they would fight to reclaim their lives.

The future was uncertain, the dangers ever-present. But they were ready to face whatever came their way. The game was far from over, but they were determined to play it on their own terms. And as they prepared for the battles ahead, they knew one thing for sure: they would never give up. They would fight, they would survive, and they would win.

Chapter 11: Release and Revenge

The courtroom was a blur of sounds and faces, but the words that echoed loudest in Rose and Alexis's ears were "Released on bail." They had been trapped in that hellhole long enough. Stepping out into the bright sunlight, the world seemed both familiar and foreign. The streets they knew so well now felt like a battlefield.

Rose took a deep breath, the city air filling her lungs with a mix of freedom and the grit of reality. "We free, Lexi. But this ain't over."

Alexis nodded, her eyes scanning the surroundings with newfound wariness. "We gotta get back on our feet, Rose. Can't let Marcus think he's won."

They walked through the streets, the familiar sights and sounds now tinged with a sense of urgency. They headed to a rundown motel where they could lay low and plan their next move. The room was small and dingy, but it was safe. For now.

Rebuilding their lives wasn't easy. They had lost everything in the fallout with Marcus. The money, the connections, the safety—they were all gone. Rose and Alexis hustled to scrape together whatever they could, taking on odd jobs and relying on the few friends they still had left.

One night, as they sat around the small table in their motel room, Rose laid out her plan. "We gotta take Marcus down, once and for all. We can't just hide and hope he forgets about us. He's too dangerous."

Alexis nodded, her jaw set with determination. "What's the plan, Rose? We ain't got much, but we gotta use what we have."

Rose spread out a map of the city, marking locations with a pen. "We hit him where it hurts. His money, his operations. We expose him for what he is. And we get Jai out."

Alexis's heart ached at the mention of Jai. She knew her friend was suffering, trapped in a nightmare. "How we gonna do that?"

Rose's eyes blazed with resolve. "We gather evidence. We get proof of his dealings, his abuses. We take it to the authorities. But first, we need to get close. We need to get inside his operations."

The first step in their plan was to reconnect with old allies. They reached out to Big Dee, who had connections and influence. Meeting in a dimly lit bar, Rose laid out their plan.

"Big Dee, we need your help. Marcus is a menace, and he's got our girl trapped. We need to take him down."

Big Dee listened, her expression serious. "Y'all got guts, comin' to me with this. But I respect that. I'll help. But it's gonna be dangerous."

Rose nodded. "We know the risks. But we can't let him keep doin' this. We need to stop him."

With Big Dee's help, they started gathering intel. They found out where Marcus was operating, who his key players were, and how his business ran. It was a dangerous game, but they had no choice.

One night, as they staked out one of Marcus's clubs, Alexis spotted Jai. She looked thinner, more fragile, but there was a glimmer of hope in her eyes when she saw them. They couldn't make contact, not yet, but seeing Jai strengthened their resolve.

"We gotta move fast," Rose said, her eyes fixed on Marcus's club. "We get the evidence, and we get Jai out. No more waiting."

They spent weeks gathering proof, using hidden cameras and recording devices. They documented the abuse, the illegal deals, the human trafficking. It was dangerous work, but they were relentless.

The night of the raid, Rose and Alexis were ready. They had given all the evidence to the authorities, and now it was time to act. They watched from a distance as the police stormed Marcus's operations, the sounds of sirens and shouts filling the air.

Marcus was caught off guard, his empire crumbling around him. Rose and Alexis moved in, their hearts pounding. They found Jai, bruised and scared but alive.

"Jai, we're getting you outta here," Alexis whispered, hugging her friend tightly.

Jai sobbed with relief. "I thought I was done for, Lexi. I thought he'd kill me."

Rose looked at the chaos around them, a sense of grim satisfaction washing over her. "We did it. We took him down."

The aftermath was a whirlwind. Marcus was arrested, his operations dismantled. Rose, Alexis, and Jai were finally free, but the scars of their ordeal remained. They had lost so much, but they had gained something more valuable—each other.

As they sat in their small apartment, the city lights twinkling outside, Rose spoke softly. "We did it. We're free. But we gotta stay sharp. There's always another threat."

Alexis nodded, her eyes filled with determination. "We survived, Rose. We'll keep surviving. Together."

Jai, still recovering, managed a smile. "We're stronger now. We can face anything."

The future was uncertain, the road ahead still filled with challenges. But they had faced the worst and come out stronger. They were a family, bound by their struggles and their triumphs. And as they looked to the future, they knew one thing for sure—they would never let anyone tear them apart again.

The game was far from over, but they were ready. They had each other, and that was enough. For now, they were free, and they would fight to keep it that way. The night was dark, the future uncertain, but their resolve was unbreakable. They had won this battle, and they were ready for whatever came next.

Chapter 12: The Heist

The dim light of the warehouse flickered, casting eerie shadows on the walls. Rose and Alexis stood at the center, surrounded by the motley crew they had assembled. Each member had a reason to hate Marcus, a grudge that needed settling.

"Listen up," Rose said, her voice cutting through the tension. "This ain't just 'bout the money. This 'bout sending a message. We hit Marcus where it hurts, take his cash, and leave him with nothin'."

Alexis nodded, scanning the faces of their allies. Big Dee stood tall and intimidating, a silent promise of brute strength. Skinny Pete, a tech wizard with a knack for getting into places he shouldn't. And then there was Rico, a smooth talker with connections in all the right, and wrong, places.

"We all got our roles," Alexis added, her tone firm. "Stick to the plan, and we get out clean. Any slip-ups, we all go down."

The crew murmured their agreement, the tension in the room thick enough to cut with a knife. This was it. Their shot at revenge.

The night of the heist, the air was electric with anticipation. They gathered in an alley near Marcus's main stash house, a nondescript building that held the key to his empire. Rose and Alexis led the way, their hearts pounding in unison.

"Big Dee, you and Rico cover the front. Make sure nobody gets in or out," Rose instructed. "Pete, you're with us. We need those locks cracked, fast."

Big Dee grunted in acknowledgment, his massive frame a reassuring presence. Rico flashed a confident grin. "We got this. Let's make it happen."

Pete, nervous but determined, nodded. "I'll get us in. Just gimme a few minutes."

As they approached the building, the adrenaline kicked in. Alexis kept a sharp lookout while Pete worked his magic on the locks. Within minutes, the door clicked open, and they slipped inside, moving like shadows.

The stash house was quiet, too quiet. Rose felt a chill run down her spine but pushed it aside. They had to move fast. They made their way to the basement, where Marcus's vault was hidden. Pete set to work on the vault, his fingers flying over the keypad.

"Almost there," he whispered, sweat dripping down his forehead.

Alexis and Rose stood guard, their senses on high alert. Every creak, every distant sound set their nerves on edge. Finally, with a soft beep, the vault door swung open, revealing stacks of cash and valuable items.

"We hit the jackpot," Alexis breathed, eyes wide with amazement.

Rose grinned, stuffing cash into the bags they'd brought. "Quick, grab as much as you can. We ain't got all night."

As they worked, a sudden noise made them freeze. Footsteps, heavy and deliberate, echoed through the building. Alexis's heart pounded in her chest. "We got company."

Rose nodded, her eyes narrowing. "We need to move. Now."

They finished loading the bags and started for the exit when the door slammed shut. Standing there, blocking their way, was Rico, a smug grin on his face and a gun in his hand.

"Rico, what the hell?" Rose demanded, her voice cold with anger.

Rico shrugged, his eyes gleaming with betrayal. "Sorry, ladies. Marcus made me a better offer. And I ain't one to turn down easy money."

Alexis's blood boiled. "You traitor. We trusted you."

Rico laughed, a harsh, mocking sound. "That's your mistake. Trust ain't got no place in this game."

Before they could react, the door burst open, and Marcus's men swarmed in. The room erupted into chaos, fists flying, bodies colliding. Rose and Alexis fought with everything they had, but the numbers were against them.

Big Dee barreled in, knocking a few men aside, but even his strength wasn't enough to turn the tide. Pete tried to hide, his fear evident, but he was dragged out, kicking and screaming.

Marcus stepped into the room, his presence commanding. He looked around at the wreckage, his eyes cold and calculating. "Well, well, look what we have here. Thought you could steal from me and get away with it?"

Rose spat at his feet, her eyes blazing with defiance. "This ain't over, Marcus. We'll take you down, one way or another."

Marcus laughed, a sound devoid of humor. "Brave words for a dead woman."

The fight raged on, but it was clear they were outmatched. Alexis felt a sharp pain as a fist connected with her jaw, sending her sprawling. She struggled to her feet, only to be knocked down again.

Just when all seemed lost, the sound of sirens pierced the air. The cops, tipped off by one of Rose's allies, stormed the building. Marcus's men scattered, the scene descending into pandemonium.

"Go, go!" Rose shouted, grabbing Alexis and pulling her toward the exit.

They stumbled out into the night, their breaths ragged, bodies bruised but spirits unbroken. They had lost the battle, but the war was far from over. They would regroup, rebuild, and come back stronger.

Back at their hideout, the crew regrouped, nursing their wounds and counting their losses. The betrayal stung, but it also steeled their resolve. They knew now who their real enemies were, and they were ready to fight.

"Rico's gonna pay for this," Alexis vowed, her eyes cold with determination.

Rose nodded, her expression grim. "And so will Marcus. We hit a bump, but we ain't stopping. We'll take them down, piece by piece."

The night was dark, the air filled with the promise of revenge. They had been betrayed, but they were not broken. The heist had failed, but their spirit remained unshaken. They would rise from the ashes, stronger and more determined than ever.

The game was far from over. They had lost a battle, but the war was just beginning. As they planned their next move, they knew one thing for sure—they would not rest until Marcus was brought to his knees. The streets were ruthless, but so were they. And they were ready to fight with everything they had.

Chapter 13: The Showdown

The abandoned warehouse stood silent, its shadows deep and foreboding. Alexis and Rose moved through the darkness, their footsteps echoing off the concrete walls. They knew Marcus was here. It was time to end this once and for all.

"Stay sharp, Lexi," Rose whispered, her voice tense. "This ain't gonna be easy."

Alexis nodded, her heart pounding. "I'm ready. Let's get this done."

They crept forward, their senses on high alert. The air was thick with anticipation, every creak and groan of the building setting their nerves on edge. They had come too far to back down now. They had to rescue Jai and take Marcus out, no matter the cost.

As they rounded a corner, they saw him. Marcus stood in the middle of the room, flanked by his men, a cruel smile on his face. Jai was tied to a chair, her face bruised and bloodied, her eyes filled with fear.

"Well, well," Marcus sneered. "Look who decided to join the party."

Rose stepped forward, her eyes blazing with fury. "This ends tonight, Marcus. We takin' you down."

Marcus laughed, a harsh, mocking sound. "You really think you can beat me? You ain't got what it takes."

Alexis felt her blood boil. "We'll see about that."

The tension in the room exploded as Rose and Alexis charged forward, fists flying. The room erupted into chaos, bodies clashing, shouts echoing off the walls. Marcus's men fought fiercely, but Rose and Alexis were driven by a desperate need for revenge and the determination to save their friend.

Rose swung a metal pipe, connecting with the jaw of one of Marcus's thugs. The man crumpled to the ground, blood pouring from his mouth. Alexis dodged a punch, countering with a swift kick to the ribs. The sound of breaking bones echoed through the warehouse.

Marcus watched, a twisted smile on his face. He seemed to enjoy the chaos, reveling in the violence. He stepped forward, pulling a knife from his belt. "Time to end this."

Rose saw the knife and her heart skipped a beat. "Alexis, watch out!"

But it was too late. Marcus lunged, the blade flashing in the dim light. Alexis tried to dodge, but the knife sliced across her arm, a searing pain shooting through her body. She stumbled back, clutching her wound.

Rose roared in fury, charging at Marcus. They collided, the knife clattering to the floor. They grappled, each trying to gain the upper hand. Marcus was strong, but Rose fought with the strength of desperation. She landed a brutal punch to his gut, doubling him over.

"Get Jai!" Rose shouted to Alexis, her voice strained with effort.

Alexis nodded, ignoring the pain in her arm. She rushed to Jai, quickly untying the ropes that bound her. "We gotta get you outta here."

Jai nodded weakly, her eyes filled with gratitude. "I thought I was done for, Lexi."

"We ain't leavin' without you," Alexis said, helping her to her feet. "Let's go."

But as they turned to leave, Marcus broke free from Rose's grip, a wild look in his eyes. He lunged for Alexis, knocking her to the ground. Jai screamed, trying to pull him off, but he was too strong.

Rose grabbed the knife from the floor, her heart pounding in her chest. She couldn't let Marcus win. With a primal scream, she charged at him, the knife raised high. Marcus turned just in time to see the blade coming down, his eyes widening in shock.

The knife plunged into his chest, and he staggered back, a look of disbelief on his face. He clutched the wound, blood pouring through his fingers. "This... ain't over," he gasped, before collapsing to the floor.

Rose stood over him, her chest heaving, the knife still clutched in her hand. She looked at Alexis and Jai, relief flooding through her. "It's over. We did it."

The aftermath was a blur of sirens and flashing lights. The police arrived, taking Marcus's men into custody. Rose, Alexis, and Jai were escorted to safety, their ordeal finally over.

At the hospital, they were treated for their injuries. Jai was weak but alive, her spirit unbroken. Alexis's arm was bandaged, the wound a painful reminder of the battle they had fought. Rose was bruised and battered, but her eyes shone with a fierce determination.

"We did it, Lexi," Jai whispered, her voice filled with emotion. "We really did it."

Alexis nodded, tears streaming down her face. "We're free, Jai. We're finally free."

Rose sat beside them, her hand resting on Alexis's shoulder. "We survived. That's what matters. But we gotta stay strong. There's always gonna be another fight."

They knew the road ahead wouldn't be easy. The scars of their ordeal would take time to heal. But they had each other, and that was enough. They had faced the worst and come out stronger. The streets were still dangerous, but they were ready.

As they left the hospital, the sun was rising, casting a warm glow over the city. The future was uncertain, but their resolve was unbreakable. They had won this battle, and they were ready for whatever came next.

The game was far from over, but they were determined to play it on their own terms. They had fought, they had survived, and they had won. And as they walked into the dawn, they knew one thing for sure: they would never give up. They would keep fighting, keep surviving, and keep winning.

The night was dark, the streets unforgiving, but they were stronger than ever. And together, they would face whatever came their way. The showdown was over, but their story was just beginning.

Chapter 14: Fallout

The hospital was a cacophony of sounds and smells—disinfectant, the beeping of machines, the distant murmur of nurses. Alexis lay on the stiff bed, staring at the ceiling, her arm heavily bandaged. The painkillers dulled the physical pain, but nothing could numb the emotional wounds.

Rose sat in a chair beside her, bruises darkening her face, a cut on her lip. Jai lay in the next bed, her eyes closed, her breathing shallow but steady. The three of them were silent, each lost in their own thoughts.

"Damn, Lexi," Rose finally said, breaking the silence. "We really went through it."

Alexis turned her head, meeting Rose's gaze. "Yeah. Feels like a dream. A bad one."

Jai stirred, her voice weak. "We did it, though. Marcus is gone. Ain't no one gonna hurt us like that again."

The physical toll was visible—bruises, cuts, and the exhaustion that weighed on them like a heavy blanket. But the emotional scars ran deeper. They had fought for their lives, and the cost had been high.

Days later, they were released from the hospital, but the city felt different. The streets they knew so well seemed foreign, haunted by the ghosts of their past battles. They returned to their apartment, a temporary refuge in the storm.

As they sat around the small table, the weight of their choices pressed down on them. Rose broke the silence, her voice raw. "We gotta talk about what's next. We can't keep livin' like this."

Alexis nodded, her eyes haunted. "I know. I don't wanna end up back in that life. We gotta find a way out."

Jai sighed, her eyes filled with regret. "We been through too much. I wanna leave all this behind, but it feels like it's always gonna follow us."

Rose looked at each of them, her gaze hard but filled with a rare tenderness. "We made choices, bad ones. But we can make new ones. We gotta stay strong, look out for each other. We leave this life behind, for good."

The days turned into weeks, and they worked to rebuild their lives. It wasn't easy. The money they had stolen from Marcus was gone, used to pay medical bills and basic necessities. They took on whatever jobs they could find, trying to stay under the radar.

Alexis found a job at a diner, working long hours for little pay. Rose took up work as a mechanic, her hands dirty but her heart a little lighter. Jai, still recovering, helped where she could, her spirit slowly healing.

But the past haunted them. Every loud noise, every shadow seemed to bring back memories of the violence and fear. They knew they had to keep moving forward, but the weight of their choices was always there.

One night, as they sat together, Alexis voiced what they were all thinking. "What if we can't escape it? What if this life is all we'll ever know?"

Rose shook her head, determination in her eyes. "We ain't defined by our past. We got a chance to start over. It ain't gonna be easy, but we gotta try."

Jai nodded, tears glistening in her eyes. "We owe it to ourselves. We deserve better."

As they worked to build new lives, they also reflected on the choices that had led them here. They talked late into the night, sharing stories of their childhoods, their dreams, and the mistakes they had made.

Rose, who had always been the strong one, opened up about her own past. "I made a lotta bad choices, got mixed up with the wrong people. But y'all gave me a reason to fight, a reason to be better."

Alexis nodded, her heart aching. "We all been through it. But we gotta learn from it, not let it drag us down."

Jai smiled weakly. "We got each other. That's what matters."

Their bond grew stronger, forged in the fires of their shared struggles. They knew the road ahead was long and filled with challenges, but they were determined to face it together.

One evening, as they walked through the city, they stumbled upon a small community center offering free classes and support groups. Rose's eyes lit up with a rare spark of hope. "Maybe this is what we need. A fresh start, somethin' positive."

They signed up for classes, eager to learn new skills and rebuild their lives. Alexis took a course in business management, hoping to one day open her own diner. Rose continued her work as a mechanic, dreaming of owning her own garage. Jai focused on counseling, wanting to help others avoid the pitfalls she had fallen into.

The community center became a place of refuge, a symbol of hope. They found friends and allies, people who understood their struggles and supported their dreams. Slowly, they began to heal, their lives taking on new meaning.

But the past wasn't easily forgotten. They still had nightmares, still flinched at shadows. They knew Marcus's associates were still out there, and the threat of retaliation loomed large.

One night, as they sat together, Rose voiced their shared fear. "We gotta stay ready. We can't let our guard down. Marcus may be gone, but his legacy ain't."

Alexis nodded, her resolve unshaken. "We've come too far to let fear control us. We fight if we have to, but we ain't gonna live in the past."

Jai smiled, a fierce determination in her eyes. "We're survivors. We'll face whatever comes, together."

As they looked out at the city, the lights twinkling in the darkness, they knew their journey was far from over. But they had each other, and that was enough. They had faced the worst and come out stronger. The future was uncertain, but their resolve was unbreakable.

They were ready for whatever came next, determined to build a new life, free from the shadows of their past. The streets were still dangerous, but they were stronger than ever. Together, they would face the challenges ahead, and they would never give up.

The night was dark, but the dawn was just beginning. And as they walked into the future, they knew one thing for sure: they were survivors, and they would keep fighting, keep surviving, and keep winning.

Chapter 15: New Beginnings

The apartment was small and shabby, but to Alexis, Jai, and Rose, it was a fresh start. It wasn't much, but it was theirs. The walls were thin, the neighbors loud, but it was a place to call home, a place where they could rebuild their lives away from the shadows of their past.

"Yo, Lexi, we need more paint," Jai called from the living room, her voice echoing through the empty space. "This place looks like a damn crime scene."

Alexis laughed, wiping sweat from her brow. "Yeah, I'll grab some when I head out. We gonna make this place shine, just watch."

Rose stood by the window, looking out at the bustling street below. "We made it out, but we gotta stay sharp. This fresh start don't mean shit if we fall back into old habits."

Alexis nodded, her eyes meeting Rose's. "I know. We gotta stay clean, stay focused. Ain't no way we goin' back to that life."

Jai sighed, sitting down on a paint-splattered stool. "It's hard, though. Sometimes I feel like the streets are callin' me back, like they ain't gonna let me go."

Rose walked over, placing a hand on Jai's shoulder. "We in this together, Jai. We keep each other strong."

Leaving the past behind was easier said than done. The streets had a way of pulling you back in, of reminding you of what you used to be. Every day was a struggle, a battle against the ghosts of their former lives. The temptation to slip back into old habits was always there, lurking in the background.

Alexis found a job at a local diner, the long hours and hard work a welcome distraction from her troubled thoughts. The tips were meager, the customers rude, but it was honest work. She took pride in it, knowing she was building something real, something she could be proud of.

Jai attended counseling sessions at the community center, her resolve to stay clean growing stronger with each passing day. She still had nightmares, still flinched at shadows, but she was fighting. Every day was a victory, a step away from the darkness that had once consumed her.

Rose worked as a mechanic, her hands greasy but her heart lighter. She found solace in the routine, in the sense of accomplishment that came with fixing things, making them whole again. It was a small shop, but it was honest work, and it kept her mind occupied.

Despite their efforts, the challenges were relentless. Money was tight, the bills piling up faster than they could pay them. The past had a way of catching up, of reminding them of what they had left behind. But they leaned on each other, their bond unbreakable.

One night, as they sat around the small kitchen table, Alexis voiced the fear that had been gnawing at her. "What if we can't do this? What if we ain't strong enough to leave it all behind?"

Rose looked at her, her eyes filled with determination. "We are strong enough, Lexi. We've been through hell and back. We can do this."

Jai nodded, her eyes filled with a rare confidence. "We just gotta keep fightin'. We got each other, and that's enough."

The words hung in the air, a promise to themselves and to each other. They would not go back. They would fight, they would survive, and they would build a new life, no matter how hard it got.

The days turned into weeks, and slowly, things began to fall into place. They made friends at the community center, found support in unexpected places. The past was still there, still a shadow over their lives, but they were learning to live with it, to move beyond it.

One evening, as they sat together, Jai spoke up, her voice filled with emotion. "I never thought I'd make it this far. I owe it to y'all. I couldn't have done it alone."

Alexis smiled, her heart swelling with pride. "We all in this together, Jai. We make each other strong."

Rose raised her glass, a rare smile on her lips. "To us. To survivin' and to the future."

They clinked glasses, the sound a small but powerful symbol of their unity, their resolve. They had come so far, and they were determined to keep moving forward.

Despite their progress, the road was still fraught with challenges. One night, as Alexis walked home from the diner, she felt the familiar prickle of fear. She turned to see a figure emerging from the shadows, a face she recognized all too well.

"Long time no see, Lexi," the man sneered, his eyes cold. "Thought you could just walk away from the life?"

Her heart pounded in her chest, but she stood her ground. "I ain't in that life no more. You best walk away."

The man laughed, a harsh, grating sound. "We'll see 'bout that."

She hurried home, her mind racing. She knew the past wouldn't let go easily, that they would have to fight for their new life every day. But she also knew they were stronger together, that they could face whatever came their way.

As they sat together that night, Alexis shared what had happened. Rose's eyes narrowed, her resolve hardening. "We knew it wouldn't be easy. But we ain't gonna let them drag us back."

Jai nodded, her hands trembling but her voice steady. "We fight, Lexi. We fight for our future."

The words were a vow, a promise to each other. They had come too far to give up now. They would face the challenges, the threats, the darkness. And they would do it together.

The night was dark, the future uncertain. But they were ready. They had each other, and that was enough. The game was far from over, but they were determined to play it on their own terms. They had fought, they had survived, and they would continue to fight. The streets were unforgiving, but so were they.

As they looked out at the city, they knew one thing for sure: they were stronger together, and they would never give up. They would keep fighting, keep surviving, and keep winning. The dawn was just beginning, and they were ready for whatever came next.

Chapter 16: Monique's Tragedy

The city was a beast that never slept, always hungry for more. Its streets were alive, buzzing with the hustle and grind of survival. Alexis, Rose, and Jai were no strangers to this life, but they had fought hard to carve out a new path. One night, as they sat at their favorite diner, they noticed a new face among the regulars.

Monique was young, maybe eighteen, with wide eyes that spoke of innocence but a hardened exterior that hinted at a rough life. She reminded Alexis of herself, back when she first got caught up in the game.

"Yo, you see that girl?" Alexis nodded towards Monique, who sat alone in a corner booth, staring into her coffee.

Rose glanced over, her eyes narrowing. "Yeah, I see her. She lookin' like she 'bout to make some bad choices."

Jai sighed, a sad smile on her lips. "She reminds me of us, before all the bullshit."

They decided to approach her, offering her a seat at their table. Monique was hesitant at first, but the warmth in their eyes drew her in. She sat down, her guard slowly lowering.

"Name's Alexis. This here's Rose and Jai. You new around here?" Alexis asked, her tone gentle but probing.

Monique nodded, her eyes flicking between them. "Yeah, just tryin' to get by. Ain't got no place to go."

Rose leaned in, her voice low. "We been there, girl. This city'll chew you up and spit you out if you ain't careful."

Monique's eyes filled with a mixture of fear and defiance. "I can handle myself."

Jai shook her head, her expression serious. "Ain't 'bout handlin' yourself. It's 'bout knowin' when to get out before it's too late."

Despite their warnings, Monique was drawn to the life they had left behind. The allure of fast money, the promise of excitement—it was a powerful pull. They tried to keep her close, offering her work at the diner where Alexis was employed, helping her find a safer path. But the streets had their hooks in deep.

One night, Monique showed up at their apartment, bruised and shaking. "I thought I could do it, but it's too much," she whispered, tears streaming down her face.

Alexis pulled her into a hug, her heart aching. "We told you, girl. This life ain't what it seems."

Monique sobbed, clinging to her. "I need out, but I don't know how."

Rose's eyes were fierce. "We'll help you, but you gotta listen. Ain't no halfway. You in or you out."

For a while, it seemed like Monique might make it. She worked at the diner, stayed off the streets, and leaned on them for support. But the city had a way of pulling you back in, of reminding you of what you thought you needed.

One evening, Monique didn't show up for her shift. Alexis felt a knot of dread in her stomach. She tried calling, but there was no answer. They searched for her, their hearts heavy with worry.

They found her in an alley, surrounded by dealers and thugs, her eyes glazed over from drugs. Alexis's heart broke at the sight. "Monique, what the hell you doin'?"

Monique looked up, her eyes filled with a mix of shame and defiance. "I'm sorry. I thought I could handle it."

Rose stepped forward, anger and fear warring in her eyes. "This ain't no game, Monique. You keep this up, you gonna end up dead."

But Monique was too far gone. The lure of the streets was too strong, and despite their best efforts, she slipped away, back into the life they had fought so hard to escape.

A few weeks later, they got the call. Monique had been found dead in a rundown motel, a victim of an overdose. Alexis felt like the ground had been ripped out from under her. She had seen so much death, so much pain, but this hit differently. Monique was a reminder of what could have been, a stark symbol of the brutal cycle they had managed to break free from.

At the funeral, the air was thick with grief and anger. Alexis, Rose, and Jai stood together, their faces set in grim determination. They knew they had done everything they could, but it didn't make the loss any easier.

As they walked away from the gravesite, Alexis spoke, her voice raw with emotion. "We gotta keep fightin'. For Monique, for us, for anyone else caught in this shit."

Rose nodded, her eyes hard. "We can't save everyone, but we can make damn sure we try."

Jai wiped away tears, her voice trembling but strong. "We keep each other strong. We stay together. That's how we survive."

The tragedy of Monique's death hung over them like a dark cloud, a constant reminder of the fragility of their new lives. But it also fueled their resolve, giving them a renewed sense of purpose. They had escaped the streets, but the battle was far from over.

They threw themselves into their work, into their new lives, determined to honor Monique's memory by staying clean and helping others. They volunteered at the community center, shared their stories with those who would listen, and fought to break the cycle that had claimed so many lives.

The nights were still long, the streets still dangerous, but they faced each challenge with unyielding determination. They had seen the worst, had lived through the darkest times, and they were stronger for it.

As they sat together one evening, the city lights twinkling in the distance, Alexis spoke the vow they all felt. "We ain't gonna let this life take us down. We fight, we survive, we live."

The words were simple, but they carried the weight of their shared experiences, their shared pain and triumphs. They knew the road ahead would be tough, but they were ready. Together, they would face whatever came their way, and they would keep fighting, keep surviving, keep living.

The night was dark, but they were a beacon of hope, a testament to the strength of the human spirit. They had each other, and that was enough. The game was far from over, but they were determined to win. And as they looked to the future, they knew one thing for sure: they would never give up. They would keep fighting, keep surviving, and keep winning.

Chapter 17: Final Confrontation

The city loomed around them, a never-ending labyrinth of shadows and memories. Alexis, Jai, and Rose stood on a rooftop, looking out over the streets that had both given and taken so much from them. The night was dark, the air thick with anticipation. They had come here to confront their past, to finally put the demons to rest.

"Yo, it's time," Rose said, her voice steady but laced with tension. "We gotta face this shit head-on."

Alexis nodded, her gaze fixed on the city below. "Ain't no runnin' from it. We gotta do this, for us, for Monique."

Jai stood a little apart, her arms wrapped around herself. "I'm scared, y'all. What if we can't shake this? What if it keeps pullin' us back?"

Rose stepped forward, her eyes fierce. "We stronger than that. We been through hell and back, and we still standin'. Ain't nothin' gonna break us now."

They made their way down the fire escape, moving through the alleys with a sense of purpose. They were heading to the place where it all began, the abandoned warehouse that had been the backdrop to so much pain and violence. It was time to face the ghosts that haunted them.

The warehouse was dark, the air thick with the scent of decay. Memories flooded back as they stepped inside, each corner a reminder of battles fought and lost. Alexis felt her heart race, but she pushed the fear down. This was their final confrontation, their chance to lay the past to rest.

"Remember when we first met?" Alexis said, her voice echoing through the empty space. "We was just kids, thinkin' we could take on the world."

Jai nodded, her eyes misty. "We ain't know nothin' 'bout what was comin'. We thought we was invincible."

Rose walked over to a broken window, staring out at the night. "We made choices, bad ones. But we did what we had to do to survive."

They stood in silence, each lost in their thoughts. The past was a heavy burden, but they had carried it together. They had fought, bled, and suffered, but they had also found strength in each other.

Alexis turned to Jai and Rose, her voice filled with determination. "We can't change what happened, but we can decide what comes next. We ain't defined by our past. We got a future, and it's ours to shape."

Jai wiped away a tear, her voice trembling. "I don't want to be scared no more. I wanna move forward, leave all this behind."

Rose stepped forward, her hand resting on Jai's shoulder. "We will. We take it one day at a time, but we move forward. Together."

The closure they sought didn't come easy. The scars they carried, both physical and emotional, were deep. But standing there, in the place that had once been their prison, they found a measure of peace. They had faced their demons, confronted the past that had haunted them for so long.

"We gotta remember where we came from," Rose said softly. "But we don't have to let it define us."

Alexis nodded, her eyes filled with a new light. "We been through the worst, and we still here. That means somethin'. It means we strong, stronger than we ever knew."

Jai smiled, a glimmer of hope in her eyes. "We got each other. That's all we need."

As they left the warehouse, the first light of dawn began to break over the city. The future stretched out before them, uncertain but filled with possibilities. They had made peace with their past, but the journey was far from over.

They walked through the streets, their steps sure and steady. They talked about their dreams, their plans for the future. Alexis wanted to open her own diner, a place where people could come and feel safe. Jai dreamed of becoming a counselor, helping others find their way out of the darkness. Rose wanted to expand her mechanic shop, providing jobs and opportunities for those looking to start fresh.

The challenges ahead were daunting, but they faced them with a renewed sense of purpose. They had survived the streets, the violence, and the betrayals. They had come out the other side, stronger and more determined than ever.

That evening, as they sat on the steps of their apartment building, watching the city come alive with lights and sounds, they knew they were ready. Ready to leave the past behind, ready to embrace the future.

"We gonna be alright," Alexis said, her voice filled with conviction. "We got each other, and that's all that matters."

Rose nodded, a rare smile on her lips. "We been through hell, but we made it out. We survivors."

Jai leaned back, looking up at the stars. "We gonna make it. We got a future, and it's bright."

The night was dark, but the dawn was just beginning. They had faced their demons, made peace with their past, and now they were ready to move forward. Together, they would build a new life, filled with hope and possibility.

The streets were still there, a constant reminder of what they had overcome. But they were no longer bound by them. They were free, and they were ready to embrace whatever came next. They had fought, they had survived, and they would continue to fight. The game was far from over, but they were playing it on their own terms. And as they looked to the future, they knew one thing for sure: they would never give up. They would keep fighting, keep surviving, and keep winning.

Chapter 18: Sad Closure

The cemetery was quiet, the air heavy with sorrow. The trio stood around Monique's grave, the stark white headstone a harsh reminder of the life they had left behind. Monique's death was a wound that hadn't healed, a constant ache in their hearts.

"Can't believe she's gone," Alexis whispered, her voice thick with grief. "She was just a kid."

Rose nodded, her eyes fixed on the headstone. "The streets don't care how old you are. They take what they want, leave nothin' but pain."

Jai wiped away tears, her hands trembling. "We tried to save her. We did everything we could."

Alexis placed a hand on Jai's shoulder, her grip firm. "We did, Jai. But some battles you can't win. We gotta remember that."

They stood in silence, each lost in their memories of Monique. She had been so full of life, so eager to escape the darkness that had swallowed so many before her. But in the end, the streets had claimed her, just like they had claimed so many others.

As they left the cemetery, the weight of Monique's death pressed down on them. They had fought so hard to escape the life that had taken her, but the past was never far behind. It was a stark reminder of the fragility of their new lives, of the constant danger that lurked around every corner.

"She deserved better," Alexis said, her voice filled with determination. "We all do. We gotta make sure we don't end up like her."

Rose nodded, her expression grim. "We owe it to her to make somethin' of ourselves. To prove that we can rise above this shit."

Jai took a deep breath, her resolve hardening. "We move forward, for Monique. We make better lives for ourselves, for her memory."

The days that followed were filled with a sense of urgency. They threw themselves into their work, determined to honor Monique's legacy by building something better. Alexis focused on her dream of opening a diner, pouring her heart and soul into every detail. She wanted it to be a place of refuge, a place where people could feel safe and loved.

Jai continued her counseling training, her passion for helping others driving her forward. She wanted to be a beacon of hope for those who were lost, just as she had once been. She knew it wouldn't be easy, but she was ready to fight for it.

Rose worked tirelessly at the mechanic shop, her hands busy but her mind always on the future. She wanted to create a space where people could find honest work, where they could build new lives away from the streets. She was determined to make a difference, one car at a time.

Despite their efforts, the past still haunted them. Every shadow, every unfamiliar face was a reminder of the dangers they had escaped. But they leaned on each other, their bond stronger than ever. They had faced the worst and come out the other side, and they were determined to keep moving forward.

One night, as they sat together in their small apartment, they talked about Monique, about the life they had left behind.

"She was brave," Alexis said, her voice soft. "She tried to make a better life, just like we are."

Rose nodded, her eyes filled with sadness. "We can't forget her. We carry her memory with us, use it to fuel our fight."

Jai wiped away a tear, her voice trembling. "We gotta make sure no one else ends up like her. We gotta keep fighting."

The months passed, and slowly, they began to see the fruits of their labor. Alexis's diner opened to great success, a small but bustling place filled with warmth and laughter. Jai graduated from her counseling program, her heart filled with pride and a sense of purpose. Rose's mechanic shop grew, providing jobs and opportunities for those looking to start fresh.

They had built new lives, but the scars of the past were still there. Monique's death was a constant reminder of the fragility of their existence, of the dangers that still lurked in the shadows. But they faced it with determination, with a fierce resolve to honor her memory.

One evening, as they stood outside the diner, watching the city lights twinkle in the distance, Alexis spoke up. "We did it. We made it out. But we gotta keep fighting, keep pushing forward."

Rose nodded, her eyes filled with pride. "We owe it to ourselves, and to Monique. We don't stop, no matter what."

Jai smiled, a glimmer of hope in her eyes. "We're stronger together. We'll face whatever comes our way."

The night was dark, but the future was filled with possibilities. They had come so far, had faced so much, and they were ready for whatever came next. They had built new lives, but they would never forget where they came from, never forget the battles they had fought.

As they looked out at the city, they knew one thing for sure: they would never give up. They would keep fighting, keep surviving, and keep honoring Monique's memory. The game was far from over, but they were ready to play it on their own terms. Together, they would face whatever came their way, with strength, determination, and an unbreakable bond.

The night was dark, the streets still dangerous, but they had each other. And as they walked into the future, they knew they would never be alone. They would keep fighting, keep surviving, and keep winning. For Monique, for themselves, and for the future they had worked so hard to build.

Don't miss out!

Visit the website below and you can sign up to receive emails whenever Rachael Reed publishes a new book. There's no charge and no obligation.

https://books2read.com/r/B-A-WXARB-UTNUD

BOOKS 2 READ

Connecting independent readers to independent writers.

Did you love *Skip the Games*? Then you should read *Cartel Bloodline*[1] by Rachael Reed!

Cartel Bloodline: A Tale of Love, Betrayal, and Survival in the Miami Underworld

In the ruthless streets of Miami, where the Cartel controls eighty percent of the cocaine flowing through the port, power is everything, and trust is a luxury no one can afford. When the most feared gangster, Antonio Brown, falls, he leaves behind a legacy that's more explosive than anyone could've imagined. His death unearths a hidden secret—an illegitimate son, Antonio Lewis, who's about to step into a world where loyalty is bought with blood and betrayal lurks around every corner.

Antonio Lewis, raised far from the chaos of Miami's underworld, gets pulled into the Cartel's deadly embrace when he learns of his father's

---

1. https://books2read.com/u/4jpKMk

2. https://books2read.com/u/4jpKMk

empire. Thrown into a cutthroat game where every ally is a potential enemy, Antonio must navigate the treacherous waters of his father's legacy, battling for his place in the empire while uncovering the dark secrets that threaten to consume him.

Lea, a deadly beauty with a heart of steel, leads The Get Money Girls, a crew of contract killers who live by their own rules. When her cousin falls in a botched hit on the Cartel, Lea vows revenge, unaware that her heart would soon become entangled with the enemy. Antonio and Lea's worlds collide in a storm of passion and deceit, their forbidden love a ticking time bomb ready to explode.

As alliances crumble and enemies close in, Antonio and Lea must face the ultimate betrayal from within their ranks. The lines between love and loyalty blur, and survival becomes a deadly game of cat and mouse. The streets of Miami become a battlefield, where every decision could mean life or death, and the only way out is to fight until the last breath.

Will Antonio rise to claim his father's throne, or will the legacy of the Cartel drag him down into the abyss? Can Lea reconcile her thirst for vengeance with the love that binds her to Antonio, or will the secrets they uncover tear them apart forever?

Cartel Bloodline is a gritty, suspense-filled journey through the dark underbelly of Miami, where power is fleeting, love is dangerous, and the ultimate betrayal could come from the person you trust the most. In this world, nothing is as it seems, and the streets never forget.

Also by Rachael Reed

Codefendant
Codefendant
Once a Cheater
Once a Cheater
Passport Bro
What Happens in Prison
Preference
Sprinkle Sprinkle
Championship Bad
Street Exodus
Street Exodus
Street Royalty
Pawns of Power
SIS
Cartel Bloodline
Get Money Girls
Skip the Games
Til Death Do Us Part
Backpage Hustle